Bridesmaids
Club

Bridesmaids Club

Wedding Day Drama

Posy Diamond

Special thanks to Linda Chapman.
With thanks to Inclusive Minds for connecting us
with their Inclusion Ambassador network,
in particular Emma Zipfel for her input.

ORCHARD BOOKS

First published in Great Britain in 2021 by The Watts Publishing Group

13 5 7 9 10 8 6 4 2

Text copyright © Orchard Books 2021
Illustrations copyright © Orchard Books 2021
The moral rights of the author and illustrator have been waived.

A CIP catalogue record for this book
is available from the British Library.

ISBN 978 1 40836 098 9

Printed and bound in Great Britain by Clays Ltd, Elcograf S.p.A

The paper and board used in this book are made from wood from responsible sources.

Orchard Books
An imprint of
Hachette Children's Group
Part of The Watts Publishing Group Limited
Carmelite House
50 Victoria Embankment
London EC4Y 0DZ

An Hachette UK Company
www.hachette.co.uk
www.hachettechildrens.co.uk

Contents

Chapter One

The smell of lunch wafted out of the school lunch hall, making Emily's tummy rumble as she headed towards the doors. It felt like ages since breaktime and Friday was always the best day for school dinners!

"Wait up, Em!"

Looking round, Emily saw her three best friends, Sophie, Cora and Shanti. Emily waited for them as they dodged around the stream of chattering younger children who had finished their lunch. "Hi," Emily greeted them.

"Are you excited?" Sophie asked.

Emily frowned and tucked her curly black hair behind her ears, as they all went into the lunch hall. "Excited? What about?"

"The school play, silly!" said Sophie, as if it was obvious. Her gaze flicked to the big clock up on the wall. "In just half an hour, Mr Burnham will tell us what the summer play will be this year!"

"I hope it's a good one," said Cora.

"I want it to have lots of dancing," said Shanti, doing a pirouette that made her long, dark brown hair fly out.

"We should get main parts this year now we're in Year Six," said Sophie happily. She nudged Emily. "I bet *you'll* get a good part. After all, Mr Burnham will be a member of your family when he marries your Uncle Mike."

Emily rolled her eyes at her friend. "As if Mr B would let that make a difference. You know he doesn't have favourites. He's always really fair. And anyway," she shrugged, "I don't really want a big part. I'm happy just painting the scenery."

She found speaking on stage a bit scary.

"Mr B's given you the best role ever already, Em," said Cora, picking up a lunch tray as they reached the serving area and waited their turn.

"What do you mean?" asked Emily, puzzled.

"Being bridesmaid at his wedding of course!" said Cora with a grin.

Emily grinned back. "OK, that *is* the best role ever!" All her friends had been bridesmaids in the last year – Sophie for her mum and dad; Shanti for her older sister and Cora for her dad and step-mum, Helena. Emily had helped out at all three weddings and at long last, it was

her turn to be a bridesmaid.

"How are the wedding plans going?" Shanti asked once they had got their food and sat down at a table. "Is there anything you need the Bridesmaids Club's help with?"

When they had found out they were all going to be bridesmaids, the four of them had formed the Bridesmaids Club. The aim of the club was to make sure that the weddings they were involved with ran smoothly. Being a bridesmaid wasn't just about wearing a pretty dress; bridesmaids had to make sure that the wedding was perfect!

"Are there any problems that need

solving?" Sophie asked eagerly.

"Not at the moment," said Emily. "But that will probably change. Something always seems to need sorting out when it comes to weddings."

Shanti nodded. "We've had to help fix things at every wedding we've been to this year – making up a special dance routine for my sister . . ."

"Making sure my step-mum wasn't scared of the horses taking her to her wedding," put in Cora.

"Even organising a whole surprise wedding for my parents on the beach!" added Sophie. "Whatever goes wrong, Em, we'll be here to help!"

They carried on talking about the weddings they'd been part of all through lunch. It was their favourite topic of conversation! After they had cleared their plates they went to the classroom where the meeting for the school play was being held. All of Year Six and Year Five would be involved in the play, but the people who wanted a bigger part had to audition. There were already ten boys and girls in the room when they arrived.

Mr Burnham – who was tall with dark brown hair, blue eyes and a closely-shaved beard – welcomed them in. "Well, hello, girls, lovely to see you. Come in and sit down. We'll just wait five more

minutes and then we'll get started."

"What's the play going to be, Mr B?" asked Cora as she perched on a desk.

He tapped his nose mysteriously. "Aha."

"I think it's going to be *The Lion King*," called one of the boys.

"*Grease!*" shouted one of the girls.

"*Shrek!*" said Cora.

Mr B grinned. "You can keep guessing all you like," he teased, "but I'm not going to tell you until everyone is here and we start the meeting."

When twenty children had crowded into the room, Mr B clapped his hands and everyone fell silent. "It's absolutely

great to see so many of you," he began. "As you know, this meeting is for those of you who would like a speaking or solo singing part. I'm going to be holding the auditions next week. If you want to be involved, you need to write your name on this sheet."

He held up a piece of paper with a table printed on it. Along the top were the names of characters. "Tick the parts you'd like to audition for. Some parts involve singing a solo – they're marked with a star. Only tick those if you're happy to sing on your own. Now." He looked round at the expectant faces. "I guess you'd all like to know what the

play is going to be? Well, it's . . . drum roll please . . ."

Everyone started a drum roll with their hands on their knees.

Mr B waited for a moment for the sound to build. "*Sleeping Beauty!*" he announced.

There was a chorus of excited gasps from most people in the room, but Cora groaned. "*Sleeping Beauty?* Mr B, that's really boring." A few of the boys nodded in agreement with her.

"*Sleeping Beauty* is not boring!" cried Mr B. "Not the version I've written anyway. Yes, there are the traditional parts of Sleeping Beauty and the Prince,

but there are also going to be lots of funny scenes in it, a bit like a panto. There'll be a dame – that's a boy dressed up as an old woman – and her two sidekicks, Billy and Bobby, and then there's the wicked fairy. She's a brilliant part – a real villain who stamps and stomps, so we need someone who will get the audience booing and hissing whenever she comes on."

"I'll audition for that!" said Cora immediately.

"There are lots of great parts. As well as the wicked fairy, there are the good fairy godmothers," said Mr B.

"Ooh, a fairy godmother would be a

fun part to play," said Sophie.

"I'm going to audition to be Sleeping Beauty or a fairy godmother," said Shanti excitedly. "What about you, Em?"

"Um," Emily stalled, adjusting her glasses. She was beginning to wonder if she wouldn't just be happiest being in the background.

"Here's the list," said Mr B, passing it round. "Sign up and I'll work out an audition schedule."

"What will we have to do at the auditions?" one of the boys asked.

"We'll do some acting together, and if you want a singing part then you'll need to prepare a song – it can be anything

you like," said Mr B.

Everyone chattered excitedly as the list was handed round.

Sophie, Shanti and Cora wrote their names down then Cora handed the sheet to Emily.

"You know, I think I might just see if I can help with the scenery instead . . ." Emily began.

"Oh, no you won't!" said Cora immediately. "It'll be much more fun if we all do the show and can rehearse together. You have to audition for a proper part."

"Yes, please audition, Em!" said Shanti. "I'm sure you'll get a part."

"Why don't you just audition to be a fairy godmother like me?" said Sophie persuasively.

"OK." Emily didn't want to miss out on being with her friends. "I'll audition

then." She wrote her name down in the fairy godmother column.

Sophie hugged her. "Yay! We can all practise for the auditions together. This is going to be so much fun!"

Chapter Two

Emily was sitting at her kitchen table finishing a picture of a snow leopard for a homework project on endangered animals when there was a knock on the front door.

"I'll get it! It'll be Uncle Mike!" her mum called from her little study that led

off the hall. Emily and her mum lived
in a terraced house, not far from school.
Emily's parents had divorced six years
ago. Now Emily lived with her mum in
the week and spent every other weekend
and some of the school holidays at her
dad's house. He lived in the same town
as them – Easton-on-Sea – so it was
easy to stay at his. She could still see all
her friends and pop back home if she'd
forgotten something. Luckily, her mum
and dad got along pretty well. She knew
some people at school with divorced
parents who fought a lot. She was glad
her mum and dad were friendly with
each other, although it did sometimes

make her wonder why they had ever split up.

Emily heard the sound of softly playing classical music as her mum opened her study door. Then she heard the front door opening and her uncle greeting her mum. Putting down her pencil, she went into the hall to say hi.

"Emily!" Uncle Mike held his arms wide when he saw her. He was tall like Emily and her mum and had the same warm, determined eyes, but he didn't have masses of curly hair like they did – his head was closely shaved. "How's my favourite niece today?"

"I'm your *only* niece," Emily said with

a smile as she hugged him. She loved
Uncle Mike. He and her mum ran an
advertising agency together so she saw
him lots. She didn't remember the time
when her parents had split up very well,
but she did remember her uncle taking
her out for lots of day trips to the cinema
and to amusement parks and then

helping her and her mum move to their new house. He was quiet and kind – and very good at listening when she wanted to talk.

Mum smiled. "Come on through and I'll make us a cup of tea. Supper's already in the oven."

Mmmm. Emily could smell the spicy stew chicken cooking and her tummy rumbled. It was her absolute favourite dinner and always reminded Emily of visiting her grandma in Jamaica.

"What time will Alex be here?" asked Mum.

"He shouldn't be long. He's just finishing off some marking," said Uncle

Mike, following Emily and her mum into their neat kitchen. The bright red pans matched the red-and-white tiles on the wall behind the cooker and the stripy mugs that hung from a mug tree. Emily's mum loved things being ordered and tidy.

"Perfect," she said, putting the kettle on and taking three mugs down. "Dave will get here about then too. He's bringing dessert with him."

"Yum!" said Emily. Her mum's boyfriend, Dave, was a brilliant baker. He and her mum had been going out for about three years. Emily really liked him. He often helped her with her maths

homework or played card games with her when her mum had to work in the evenings. He'd even taught her how to make his grandmother's Nigerian pound cake. She was glad he was coming round – it would make it less awkward having Mr B over.

Even though Uncle Mike and Mr B had been going out for two years and had been engaged for six months, it still felt weird having a teacher in the house. She was very glad Mr B wasn't her class teacher at school. That would have been even more awkward! Luckily, Mr B taught Year Three so she didn't usually see much of him. Though that would

change if she did the play, she realised.

"That's a great drawing, Em," said Uncle Mike, looking at Emily's picture.

"Thanks," said Emily. Art was her favourite subject. Her dad owned an arts and craft shop in the centre of town and she loved to help out there when she stayed with him. She cleared away her books and then sat down at the table with her mum and uncle.

"I'm really looking forward to seeing the hotel tomorrow," Mum said. "What's it like?"

"Big," said Uncle Mike. "Very grand. Just between us, I'd have chosen somewhere smaller for the wedding if it

had been left to me, but you know what Alex is like – the more dramatic, the better! As soon as he saw it, he said we simply had to get married there."

"Do you need a hand with anything to do with the wedding?" asked Emily, remembering what her friends had said. "The Bridesmaids Club can help if there's anything that needs doing."

"Thanks, sweetie, but it's all under control at the moment," said Uncle Mike. "The hotel is dealing with the catering and the cake. We've booked a car, ordered flowers and bought wedding outfits for ourselves and for our best woman of course . . . " He threw a grin at Mum. Instead of having a best man at the wedding, Uncle Mike and Mr B had asked Mum to be their best woman. "We'll get the menu finalised tomorrow at the hotel and then we can start looking for bridesmaid dresses for you, Em. Alex thought something in lilac would go with the purple and gold colour theme. Does that sound OK to you?"

"Yes!" Emily said eagerly. She loved lilac. They talked about the wedding until Dave arrived with a pound cake, the soft sponge drizzled with a layer of white icing.

"Oh, wow!' said Emily, her mouth

watering. She reached up to pick a crumb off the plate.

"Fingers off, missy." Dave softened his words with a warm smile. "This is for later. No snacking." He put it down on the side.

Mum groaned. "I'll never fit into my wedding suit if you keep making cakes like that."

Dave kissed her. "Me neither. I promise I'll make a fruit salad next time!"

There was a knock at the door and Uncle Mike went to let Mr B in.

"Hello, all!" Mr B said loudly as he came into the kitchen. With his tall frame and booming voice, he always

seemed to fill every space he was in. "Hi again, Emily."

"Hi," she muttered shyly, feeling herself start to blush. It was so weird having a teacher in her kitchen.

"Emily, can you get Alex a drink?" Mum asked. "There's wine or ginger beer or a cup of tea."

"Sure, what would you like to drink Mr B . . . Al— . . . er?" Emily stuttered. Mr B had told her to call him Alex outside school but she just couldn't get used to it. Her cheeks grew hotter.

"You don't have to call him Mr B, Emily," said Uncle Mike, chuckling. "You're not at school now."

"It's fine. I'll answer to anything," said Mr B, waving a hand. "I'll have some ginger beer please. So, what did you think about my choice for the school play?" he asked as Emily poured him a glass out of the big jug of homemade ginger beer. "Are you looking forward to performing?" His face split into a happy beam. "I was delighted when you said you were going to audition. It's fabulous to see you putting yourself forward for a change. Well done you!"

Emily felt a warm, happy rush at the praise.

"You're auditioning for the school play?' Uncle Mike said to her in surprise.

"I thought you didn't like acting."

"Sophie, Cora and Shanti are all going to audition," Emily explained. "So, I said I would too."

"You'll love it!" said Mr B confidently. "Being up on stage with everyone watching you – there's nothing like it."

"Yeah," Emily said doubtfully.

Dave chuckled. "I remember when I was in my school play. I had so little talent they asked me to be a tree. All I had to do was stand there with my arms out. That suited me just fine."

"Maybe I could be a tree?" said Emily hopefully to Mr B.

Mr B waved his arms. "Oh, no. You

want a speaking part, I'm sure."

Uncle Mike glanced at Mum. "Do you remember when we did *Aladdin* at school and I was picked to be the genie? I was fine in rehearsals, but on the night I got so nervous because of everyone watching that I forgot all my lines. It was so embarrassing! The teacher had to whisper the lines to me. Then I forgot which side of stage to come on from when Aladdin rubbed the lamp. He just kept rubbing and rubbing until someone in the audience shouted, 'he's behind you!'"

"I do remember it," said Mum, chuckling. "It was hilarious. The

audience fell about laughing."

"I just wanted the floor to open and swallow me up," said Uncle Mike. "That was it. I've never been on stage since."

Emily thought how awful it would be to get everything wrong with a hall full of people watching you. "Maybe I shouldn't audition," she said uneasily. "Maybe I should just help backstage."

"No, no, no!" exclaimed Mr B. "You'll be fine. More than fine – you'll be wonderful!"

"When are the auditions, Alex?" asked Mum.

"On Tuesday," said Mr B. "I'm going to get everyone together in the hall to

try acting out some scenes. Those who want singing parts can sing and then, best of all, they'll all get to play some improv games!"

"Improv?" echoed Emily, wondering what she'd let herself in for.

"Improvisation. It means making things up on the spot," explained Mr B. "I give you a scenario, like you're

trapped in a lift or someone has just spilled something over you in a café, and you just start acting. It's a great way to show off your creativity – you'll love it!"

It didn't sound like the kind of thing Emily would love at all. Butterflies began to flap in her tummy, making her feel sick. She had thought auditioning would just mean reading out a few lines in a classroom to Mr B. Having to make stuff up and act in front of everyone sounded much more scary. She handed Mr B his drink and sat down anxiously. She was beginning to wonder if she should have agreed to audition after all!

Chapter Three

"Are you OK?" Mum asked Emily the next morning as they drove to Langton Hall – the hotel where Uncle Mike and Mr B were going to get married. "You've been really quiet since supper yesterday."

"I'm . . . I'm OK," Emily muttered. But she wasn't. She was worrying about the

audition. She really didn't want to stand up in front of everyone and improvise. Ever since Mr B had said that, she'd been wondering if she could possibly get out of it. The trouble was Sophie, Cora and Shanti would be upset if she didn't audition and she didn't want to disappoint Mr B either. *I don't know what to do,* she thought.

Her mum glanced over at her again. "You're not OK, are you, Em? I can tell something's bothering you. Are you worried about being a bridesmaid? Or about Mr B becoming your uncle? You were fine until he arrived yesterday."

"No! It's nothing to do with him or the

wedding!" Emily burst out.

"So, there is *something* wrong then," said her mum.

Emily sighed. "Yes, but it's not the wedding. It's the play," she admitted. "I'm scared about auditioning. What if I look really stupid, Mum? What if when I'm supposed to be acting I just freeze?"

"Oh, Em," said her mum. "Is it really just that?" She looked relieved as Emily nodded. "Look, I'm sure the audition won't be nearly as bad as you're thinking. How about you invite the others round later, tell them you're worried and see if they can help you practise for it." She smiled. "Your friends

are always very good at helping out."

"Can I really ask them to come round?" said Emily, perking up. "Could they sleep over?"

"Yes, that's fine," said her mum.

Emily took out her phone and immediately texted her friends.

Do you want to sleep over at mine tonight and practise for the auditions? I'm feeling nervous.

The replies pinged back along with emojis of sweets, party poppers and thumbs up.

Deffo!

Count me in!!! We can practise acting together, stay up really late and eat

sweets all night long!!!

Don't be nervous, you'll be great! xxx

Emily felt a rush of happiness as she put her phone back in her pocket. Her friends were the best!

Langton Hall stood at the end of a long, sweeping driveway with oak trees on either side. It was a huge old mansion built of golden stone that had been converted into a luxury hotel. The entrance was flanked by stone pillars that had red roses scrambling over them, and three wide steps led up to the door.

"Wow! This really is something special," said Mum as she and Emily got out of the car. Their feet crunched on the gravel as they walked up to the imposing front door.

"It's like one of the houses in that TV programme with the butlers and maids you sometimes watch," said Emily, in awe. She began to wonder if she should have worn something smarter. "Did you and Dad get married somewhere fancy like this?"

Her mum laughed. "Definitely not. We got married at the registry office and then went for a meal with our friends and close family at a restaurant in town.

We'd only just finished at art college and hardly had any money but we didn't care. We were so in love!" A faraway smile caught her lips as she remembered. For a moment she looked lost in her memories.

"If you loved each other so much, why did you split up?" Emily asked. "I mean, could you . . . would you . . ." The words died on her tongue. She wanted to ask if they would ever get back together, but she couldn't quite get the words out.

Her mum seemed to guess what she was thinking. She shook her head. "Oh no, Em. Don't go thinking your dad and I might one day get back together.

I can tell you for certain that is not going happen. We did love each other very much once, but that's all in the past." She reached out and squeezed Emily's hand. "Sometimes people love each other but they aren't suited to living together and eventually make each other unhappy. Your dad and I are too different. We get on much better apart."

"Why?" Emily still didn't understand.

"You know how messy and disorganised your dad is? It drove me mad," Mum said. "I know it sounds a small thing, but when you live with someone, something like that can become a big deal. And I could

never rely on him. He'd promise to do something and then get distracted by an art project or something he wanted to photograph. I'd come home from work and find you were still in your pyjamas and the house was a mess. You probably don't remember it, but we argued all the time. Dave and I are a much better match and I'm sure one day your dad will meet someone who suits him much better too."

Emily managed a smile. "Dad *is* kind of messy. He hasn't changed."

"I know," her mum said gently. "And that's why we don't work well as a married couple. But even though we

may not love each other any more, we're still friends and we both really love you. You know that, don't you?"

Emily nodded. "Do you think you'll get married again one day, Mum?" she asked, thinking about Dave.

"Maybe," said Mum with a smile. "But for now we have another wedding to focus on." She pointed to a bright yellow car that was coming up the drive. "It looks like your uncle and uncle-to-be are here."

Mr B parked his car and jumped out along with Uncle Mike.

"Oh my goodness. Isn't this place amazing?" Mr B said, sweeping his arm

around. "I can just see purple and yellow flowers cascading down the steps, waiters handing out glasses of champagne and tiny delicious canapes . . ."

"Canapes, now you're talking!" said Uncle Mike, patting his tummy. "Do you think we'll get to sample any of their cooking today when we choose the wedding menu?"

They all headed up the steps and through the front door. There was a huge hallway with an enormous crystal chandelier and old portraits displayed on the walls. A woman in a smart blue suit was standing behind an antique desk. Emily wondered if she would be snooty,

but she greeted them with a welcoming smile. "Hello, may I help you?"

"We're here to meet with Cheryl, the wedding organiser," said Mr B. He took Uncle Mike's hand. "We're getting married next month."

"Of course. Come with me," said the woman. "Cheryl's in the morning room." She led them through the hotel, pointing out the grand old hall with panelled walls where the ceremony would take place and then leading them into a high-ceilinged room filled with comfortable green-and-pink sofas and armchairs. French windows opened out on to the immaculate formal gardens.

Cheryl, the wedding organiser, stood up to greet them and soon they were deep in discussion about arrangements for the wedding.

After a while, Cheryl nodded to a hovering waiter dressed in a red waistcoat and dark grey trousers. He disappeared and came back bearing a silver tray filled with delicious canapés. There were little pancakes covered with orange strips of smoked salmon, pieces of tender chicken on tiny skewers, white china spoons with prawns on them and tiny beef pies. But it was the mini cheeseburgers that caught Uncle Mike's attention the most.

"Now these look good!" he said, helping himself to one. "Burgers are my favourite food!" He munched. "Mmm," he said, nodding. "We've definitely got to have these!"

Cheryl made a note. "So, we'll serve canapés while the guests mingle and then you were planning a buffet for the meal?" She broke off as a fire alarm started blaring out. They all covered their ears with their hands.

"Goodness me, I don't know what's going on," shouted Cheryl above the noise. "I didn't think there was a fire drill planned for today. We'd better go outside in case it's a real fire!"

They headed out through the French windows and gathered on the lawn with the other staff and guests. The alarm stopped and a chef came running out, dressed all in white. "I'm so sorry. One of the ovens is playing up. It's under control now. You can go back inside."

"How dramatic!" said Mr B.

"We can stay out here for a while," said Cheryl. "Let me show you where you can have your photos taken."

She showed them round the grounds of Langton Hall. The gardens were stunning. There were beds of roses just starting to come into bloom and beautifully kept rockeries where pink

56

and purple flowers tumbled over stones. The grass was perfectly mown in stripes. There was even an arch covered with white summer jasmine that the grooms could stand under for their photos.

"This is all just perfect!" exclaimed Mr B happily.

"I'd have been happy with any wedding, small or big," said Uncle Mike, looking at him. "The

important thing is *who* you're marrying."
They kissed. Emily felt a wave of
happiness break over her. She'd been to
three very different weddings in the last
year and each one had been wonderful
in its own way, but she knew this one
was going to be the very best.

*I'm going to make sure Uncle Mike and
Mr B have the most perfect wedding day,* she
thought. *Nothing is going to spoil it!*

Chapter Four

After they had finished at Langton Hall,
Uncle Mike and Mr B took Emily and
her mum out for lunch at a nearby pub.
The conversation moved on from the
wedding to the school play.

"I think Emily's a bit nervous about
these auditions," Mum told Mr B as they

all tucked into big plates of scampi
and chips.

Emily shot her mum a *be-quiet* look.

"Oh, Emily, you mustn't be nervous!"
exclaimed Mr B, patting her hand. "I can
help you prepare if you like?"

"No, no, it's fine," said Emily quickly.
It would be way too embarrassing to
practise with Mr B! "Sophie, Shanti and
Cora are coming round for a sleepover
and we're going to practise together."

"So, what is it you're nervous about
exactly?" asked her mum.

"I . . . I don't know," muttered Emily,
wishing her mum would be quiet. "I
suppose it's just . . . well . . . standing up

in front of everyone on my own and everyone watching." She blushed and looked at her plate.

"That's easily solved!" said Mr B. "I'll let people audition in pairs or small groups if they want to."

"Really?" said Emily.

"Really. I'm glad you told me. Sometimes I forget that not everyone likes to be the centre of attention."

Uncle Mike grinned. "You can say that again. You love being centre stage, Alex, but I'm like Emily. I'm happiest in the background."

Mr B chuckled. "I know. Not everyone is a big show-off like me. I can't wait for

the wedding. Being centre of attention all day long – my idea of heaven! Talking of which, we need to work out how we're going to make our entrance."

Uncle Mike scratched his head. "I thought we might just walk in?"

"Oh, no!" Mr B threw his arms wide and knocked a salt cellar off the table in his enthusiasm. "I want music, drama, theatre – this is going to be a wedding that everyone remembers!"

On the way back home, Emily and Mum stopped at the supermarket and

bought some supplies for the sleepover
– popcorn, sweets, strawberries and
a massive bar of chocolate. Emily's
bedroom was too small for everyone
to sleep in so she took over the lounge.
While her mum cooked lasagne for
supper, Emily pushed the sofa and coffee
table back and got out the inflatable
mattresses from the cupboard under
the stairs. She blew up the beds and put
the popcorn into paper bowls that she
decorated by drawing stars and hearts
on them with gold pens. Then, to make
the room look more special, she made
some colourful bunting out of triangles
of old fabric glued on to ribbon and

looped it over the curtain poles. She stepped back. *Perfect.* She was ready for her friends to arrive!

"Yum!" said Sophie, licking her fingers. Dave had brought round a batch of his homemade coconut candy. The girls had taken the flaky coconut sweets into the lounge after supper and polished them off as they played one of their favourite sleepover games – Consequences. They each had to write down a boy's name then fold the paper over and hand it on to the person sitting next to them, then

they wrote a girl's name, where they had met, what they said, what they did and the consequence of it all. Each time they had written something they folded the paper over and handed it on. At the end they all read out the story on the piece of paper they were left with.

"Listen to my story!" said Cora. She unfolded it and grinned. "OK, here goes. Mr B met Beyoncé at the swimming pool. He said: "I like your hat." She said: "Watch out!" They had a jelly fight and the consequence was ... they went to Disneyland together and lived happily ever after."

They all giggled. Emily held up the

nearly empty plate of coconut sweets. "Anyone want another?"

"No thanks, I'm stuffed,' said Sophie. The others shook their heads too.

"What should we do now?" said Emily. They'd made up a dance before supper and Shanti had sung the song she was going to sing for the auditions.

"We could watch a film or play Monopoly?" suggested Sophie.

"We should practise our acting," said Cora. "After all, that's why we came round."

"OK," Emily sighed. She would have been happy just to carry on doing normal sleepover stuff.

Cora leapt to her feet and pulled her sleeping bag around her shoulders like a cloak. "Ah-ha-ha-ha!" She gave an evil laugh and tottered forward. "I am the wicked fairy godmother. Be scared of me, my pretties, be very scared!" She pointed her finger at her friends as they sat on the sofa. She hissed in a sinister voice, "I shall send you all to sleep and you will never wake up again! Never! Never! NEVER! Ah-ha-ha-ha!" Her voice rose into a shriek. She swung round, swirling the sleeping bag dramatically over her shoulders and then stalked out of the room, cackling as she went.

The others all clapped and whooped.

Cora poked her head back into the room. "Well, what do you think?" she asked in her normal voice.

"I think you'd be awesome as the wicked fairy!" said Emily. "I hope you get the part!" She really wished she could be as confident as Cora.

"You're worryingly good at being evil," said Sophie.

Cora grinned. "Well, I do have an evil stepmother to model my acting on. OK, that's not fair," she went on quickly as she saw their faces. "Helena isn't that bad. In fact, now she and Dad are married, she's kind of growing on me."

"So, you're getting along better now?"

asked Emily. For a while, Cora hadn't wanted her dad to marry Helena at all and had tried to sabotage the wedding.

Cora nodded. "She's started coming to the stables where I keep Star and having riding lessons – Mollie May too," said Cora. Mollie May was her five-year-old stepsister. "She's actually quite cute. Well, when she's talking about ponies not princesses! Now, let's try doing a scene." Cora pulled some papers from her bag. "I watched *Sleeping Beauty* with Mollie May and copied out one of the scenes from the movie, even though it won't be the same as Mr B's version."

"Brilliant!" Sophie said eagerly as

Cora handed the scripts out. In the scene, preparations were being made in the palace for Sleeping Beauty's sixteenth birthday party. There were four parts — Sleeping Beauty, the king, the queen and a governess. "Can I be Sleeping Beauty?" asked Shanti.

"Sure, I'll be the snooty governess," said Cora.

"I don't mind what part I play," said Sophie.

Emily saw that the king had the fewest lines. "I'll be the king," she said quickly. They started to act out the scene. The others threw themselves into their parts, making the most of their lines, even

Shanti who was usually quite shy, but Emily felt self-conscious and awkward. Her heart beat faster as she waited for her turn to speak. Although she could read the words perfectly well, they seemed to get mixed up in her head and she stumbled over them, gabbling the lines out as quickly as possible.

"Em, slow down!' said Sophie. "You're going way too fast."

"And speak louder," advised Cora. "You can't just mumble. You've got to really act them out. You sound like Emily, not like a king."

Emily bit her lip and looked down at the carpet. It was no good. She was

totally useless at this.

Shanti squeezed her hand. "Hey, it's OK," she said softly. Although Emily was looking down, she sensed Shanti glancing at Sophie and Cora. "Why don't we just read through the lines together so we get used to what we have to say before we start acting the scene out properly? It's really hard to just get up and do it. Unless you're Cora, of course!"

Emily shot her a grateful look.

"Good plan," said Sophie. "Come on, Em." She sat down on the sofa and patted the space next to her. "Let's all sit down and read through the lines."

Reading through the lines and not having to think about moving around was much easier. Emily gradually started to relax.

By the time they had read the scene through three times, she was feeling more confident and when they tried acting it out again, Emily didn't make nearly as many mistakes as she had in her first attempt.

Cora high-fived everyone when they had finished. "That was awesome!"

"You were loads better in that scene, Em," said Sophie.

"I guess it wasn't too hard," Emily admitted, forcing herself to smile.

"You'll be brilliant in the auditions," Shanti told her encouragingly. "I know you will."

Emily crossed her fingers and tried to believe her.

Chapter Five

The auditions were after school on
Tuesday. Mr B started by getting
everyone to play some games – standing
in a circle and throwing an imaginary
ball that changed size; passing a pretend
object from one person to another;
miming an action he gave them, such

as washing the dishes. After that, they all learned a simple dance together. It would have been good fun, but Emily was too nervous to enjoy herself. She was glad when the singing auditions started and she could just sit at the side of the hall and watch.

Shanti auditioned for a solo. She sang a song from the musical of *Matilda* and was really good. There were several other good singers, but the best was a girl called Tilly, who was in the same Year Six class as Sophie and Shanti. Tilly sang a sad song called 'Castle On a Cloud'. Her voice was so beautiful that afterwards there was a moment's silence

and then everyone broke into applause.

Mr B looked like he was wiping away a tear. "Wonderful, just wonderful, Tilly!"

"Thanks, Mr B," said Tilly, looking pleased. She hurried back to sit with her friends.

"Tilly's brilliant at acting too," Shanti whispered to Emily. "I bet she'll be picked to be Sleeping Beauty."

"I think you will be," said Emily loyally.

When the singing auditions were finished, Mr B handed out scenes for them to read through. "You can work in groups," he told them. "I'll give you ten minutes to prepare and then you can

perform them." When he reached the Bridesmaids Club, he smiled and said, "I'm imagining you lot want a scene for four people?"

"Yes please!" they chorused.

The scene he gave them had all the Fairy Godmothers in it. They split it so that Cora was the bad fairy, while Shanti, Sophie and Emily played the good fairies. Emily was relieved that she only had to say a few lines. Cora told Emily where to stand and how to say the lines, and to her surprise it wasn't that scary when they stood up and acted the scene out in front of everyone. When Cora started stamping around as

the Wicked Fairy and everyone started laughing, Emily even found herself enjoying it!

Mr B seemed pleased. He gave them all a wide smile when they finished. "Excellent, girls! Well done!"

At last it was time for them to improvise. Emily's heart beat fast as Mr B called their group up to the front. "OK, I want you to act this scene out – one of you is the mum, two of you are children and you're trying to persuade her to buy you something, and the fourth person can be the shopkeeper. You've got one minute to discuss and then off you go."

"I don't know what to do!" whispered

Emily to the others, starting to panic.

"You'll be fine," said Shanti as they huddled together. "Just imagine we're in your dad's shop, Em. You be behind the counter, I'll be the mum . . ."

"And we can be the children," said Cora. "I'll be a spoilt toddler. Sophie, you be a bored teenager."

"Ready?" called Mr. B.

"Ready!" said Shanti with a bright smile. Before Emily had time to feel nervous, they'd begun. Cora was a brilliant toddler throwing a tantrum and Sophie did a lot of eye-rolling and shrugging, while Shanti asked Emily polite questions about art supplies. All

Emily had to do was answer and pretend to be helping out in her dad's shop. It was easy!

Emily felt a tidal wave of relief as they finished. She'd done it! She'd got through the audition. She hadn't chickened out or frozen or let anyone down.

"See, it wasn't that bad, was it?" said Sophie, nudging her.

When everyone had finished, Mr B thanked them. "It's been absolutely great having you audition," he said. "I'm pleased to say there are parts for everyone. Before I give them out, I'd like to put in a plea. I need as many parents and carers as possible to help with making the scenery and costumes, so please ask your grown-ups if they would be happy to volunteer. We're going to have a scenery-building weekend in four weeks' time."

"My mum said to let you know she'd help," said one of the boys.

"Mine too!" said Tilly.

"I bet my dad will be happy to help as well," said Emily. "He loves painting and making things."

"Brilliant!" said Mr B. "The more the merrier! And if any of you would like to come and help you'll be more than welcome too. Now," he flourished the sheet of paper in front of him, "it's time

to announce the parts." He started to read out the list. "Sleeping Beauty ... Tilly!" Everyone cheered and clapped.

Emily glanced at Shanti, hoping she wouldn't be upset, but her friend was cheering and clapping along with everyone else. She caught Emily's look. "Tilly's way better than me," she said generously. "She deserved the main part."

Mr B continued with his list. Cora was the Wicked Fairy Godmother just as she'd hoped. She whooped in delight.

"And finally, our three good fairy godmothers will be played by ... Shanti, Sophie and Emily," announced Mr B, "And Shanti will sing the solo."

The girls high-fived each other in delight.

"I'll give out the scripts tomorrow," said Mr B. "I'd like you to be off the book – which means having learnt your lines – in three weeks. We'll be rehearsing every Tuesday, Wednesday and Thursday

lunchtime but you won't all be needed at every rehearsal. I'll put up a rehearsal schedule tomorrow. And that's it!" He stood up. "This is going to be the best show ever! Did you all hear that? What's it going to be?"

"The best show ever!" the cast all shouted back.

Chapter Six

Emily stood on the vast stage. Hundreds of people were sitting in the audience and they were all staring at her expectantly. Her hands were sweaty and her heart felt like it was going to burst out of her chest. What were her lines? She couldn't remember them. She couldn't even remember what play she was in! With a

strangled squeak, she started to run off stage
but then she tripped and fell on her face. The
hall filled with gales of mocking laughter . . .

Emily woke with a start, her heart
beating fast. Where were all the people?
She took a breath as she realised it
was just a nightmare. They were now
four weeks into rehearsing and Mr B
had started getting them to rehearse
without their scripts. Emily had learnt
all her lines but she just couldn't seem to
remember them when she was in front
of everyone. At the first "off the book"

rehearsal, her mind had gone blank and she'd gaped like a goldfish until Sophie had whispered the line to her. Mr B had been understanding about it.

"Don't worry," he had said to her. "Just make sure you keep on learning your lines and you'll be fine."

But Emily *had* learnt her lines. She could recite them perfectly at home – she could practically recite the whole script. She just couldn't seem to remember her lines when it mattered, when everyone was watching.

Rubbing her eyes, she got up and went downstairs.

Her mum was buttering a slice of toast.

"Morning," she said. Then she frowned. "You don't look like you slept very well."

"I didn't," Emily confessed. "I keep having nightmares about the show. I'm sure I'm going to forget my lines."

"But when you practised them with me last night, you were word-perfect," her mum said.

"I know. I can do them here with you, I just can't do them at school," Emily groaned. "I'm glad it's Saturday and we don't have a rehearsal today. I hate saying my lines in front of everyone."

"It's stage fright," her mum said. "I used to suffer from it when I had to give presentations at work. The more public

speaking you do though, the better you get at dealing with it. It's lucky you've got the play; it means you can learn how to conquer your nerves before the wedding."

"That's different," said Emily. "I don't have to talk in front of everyone when I'm a bridesmaid."

"Ah . . ." Her mum looked a bit uncomfortable. "About that . . . Uncle Mike was talking to me yesterday at work and mentioned that he and Alex were hoping that, because you are the only bridesmaid, you would read their favourite poem out during the wedding ceremony. It's only a short poem," she

went on hastily as Emily's eyes widened in horror. "Only about eight lines."

Emily shook her head hard. "No, Mum, I can't! I just can't!"

"Not even for your Uncle Mike?" her mum said. "I know it would mean so

much to him and Alex."

Emily licked her dry lips, her stomach clenching in fear at the thought. It was bad enough saying her lines in the school play with her friends beside her but at the wedding she'd be on her own in front of loads of people. *I can't do it,* she thought, but then she imagined her uncle's disappointed face.

I have to, she realised. She couldn't let him down.

"Um . . . OK," she said in a small voice. "I guess I can do it."

Her mum smiled. "Good girl. It'll make your uncle very happy and it is really good to get used to speaking in public at

your age. I wish I'd done it when I was younger."

Emily gave her a shaky smile then took her phone off the charger and quickly texted the rest of the Bridesmaids Club.

ARGH! I've got to read a poem at the wedding. I don't know what to do!!!! HEEEEEELP!!!

She pressed *send*. Within a minute, Sophie had sent a text with a line of emojis all showing a face with the mouth open and the eyes covered by hands. Shanti sent a row of question marks and then Cora's reply appeared.

We need a BC meeting!! My house

this morning? Ask if you can have lunch here before we go into school to help with the scenery this afternoon! Don't worry, Em. The BC will sort this out! Xxx

Chapter Seven

The Bridesmaids Club met in Cora's massive kitchen. It was very modern with a huge fridge and shining white units.

"I can't believe your uncle asked you to read a poem, Em," said Shanti sympathetically as they shared a pack of chocolate chip cookies. "Can't you tell

him you don't want to do it?"

"Mum said if I don't he would be really disappointed," said Emily. "Oh, what am I going to do?" Her stomach twisted with anxiety at the thought of standing up and saying a poem in front of two hundred wedding guests.

"We can help you practise it," said Cora.

"But you won't be there on the day," said Emily. She swallowed. "It wouldn't be so scary if you were all going to be beside me."

Sophie twirled the end of her ponytail thoughtfully. "Maybe you could get us invited to the wedding?"

"Can you ask?" said Shanti.

Emily sighed. "No. I asked ages ago if you could come but Uncle Mike said they're only allowed a certain number of guests at the hotel and they've already reached the maximum number. A lot of my relatives are coming over from Jamaica for the wedding."

"We could sneak in?" suggested Cora.

"Sneak in where?" asked Helena, Cora's step-mum, as she came into the kitchen. She was wearing smart dark jeans and a pink fluffy jumper. Her blonde hair bounced on her shoulders and she was carrying an armful of pastel-coloured dresses.

"To Emily's uncles' wedding," Cora explained to her.

Helena chuckled. "I don't think gate-crashing a wedding is going to make you girls very popular."

"I guess not," Cora said, sighing. "Are those costumes for the show?' She nodded at the fabric in Helena's arms.

"Yes!" Helena beamed. "I've finished making the three Fairy Godmothers' dresses," she explained to the others. "What do you think?" She shook the dresses out. There was a pink one, a peach one and a pale yellow one. They had full skirts that were covered with a layer of shimmering gauzy material and

little shoulder straps. Helena had sewn
sparkling jewels around the necklines.

"They're gorgeous!" said Emily,
wondering which one would be hers.

"Beautiful!" said Sophie, touching the skirt of the pink dress.

Cora wrinkled her nose. "They're OK for the good fairy godmothers, but I hope mine isn't going to be quite as . . . *flouncy*."

Helena raised her eyebrows. "Do you really think I'd put you in a flouncy, pink dress, Cora? Have some faith! Wait here a sec and I'll show you what I've been making for you."

She returned a few moments later with something held behind her back. "Ta-da!" she said, pulling out a glittering black and purple costume and a pair of black biker boots. "What do you

think?" The costume's skirt was made of deep purple fabric and covered in black netting that was cut in a jagged line. The bodice was made out of the same purple material decorated with black ribbons that had been sewn in swirls, and on the back there were wings made of black gauze and black sequins.

"Oh, wow!" exclaimed Cora. "I absolutely love it!"

Helena grinned. "I had a feeling you just might."

Emily felt a warm rush as she saw Helena and Cora swap smiles. It was lovely to see they were getting on better now. They'd got off to a really

tricky start, partly because they were so different. Helena worked in fashion and loved make-up and smart clothes, whereas Cora loved horses and preferred wearing jeans and trainers.

After a quick lunch of toasted sandwiches, cucumber and tomatoes, Helena drove the girls to school. Cora's dad wasn't around because he'd taken Mollie May, Cora's step-sister, to a birthday party at a farm. "Your dad wouldn't have been much use anyway," Helena said to Cora. "He's not the best at carpentry and painting."

"Definitely not," agreed Cora. "Last time he did some DIY, he tried to put a

shelf up in my room but as soon as I put books on it, it collapsed!"

They piled out of the car and helped Helena carry the costumes and her sewing machine inside.

Mr B was in the school foyer. "Wait!" he exclaimed dramatically, holding up his hand to stop them entering. "What's this I see? No school uniform, girls. You can't possibly come in!" He grinned as their faces fell. "Only joking! Come along, there's lots to be done."

"I've brought the costumes I've made so far," said Helena, gesturing to the dresses the girls were holding.

"Let's have a sneaky peek." Mr B took

the pink one from Sophie and shook it out. "Oh, this is divine!"

Helena looked really pleased. "I love making clothes but I hardly ever do it these days. This has been a great excuse to get my sewing machine out again. I'm looking forward to doing some more sewing this afternoon."

"You wouldn't fancy another commission, would you?" asked Mr B.

"What would it be?" Helena asked.

Mr B shot a look at Emily. "Well, we still need a bridesmaid dress for Emily. I've been having a look online, but I can't find anything that's exactly right."

"Oh, I'd be more than happy to make

one for her!" said Helena.

Sophie's eyes widened. "Mr B, I don't suppose you need some wardrobe supervisors for your wedding, do you?" she asked quickly. "Me, Cora and Shanti would be happy to come along and help out on the day."

Emily gave her uncle-to-be a hopeful look. Could this be a way to get her friends invited to the wedding?

But to her disappointment, Mr B shook his head. "That's a very sweet offer, Sophie, but I'm sure we'll be fine. Now, off you go, girls. There's a costume-making group in my classroom. You could join in with that or with the

prop-making gang in the library. Emily, your dad's taken charge of making the scenery, if you'd like to help with that. He's in the hall."

"We'll go and see if he needs a hand," said Emily. It all sounded fun, but she'd rather paint than anything else.

"That was a good try at getting us into the wedding," Shanti said to Sophie as they set off to the hall.

"I thought it was worth a go," Sophie said, sighing. "Too bad he didn't want us to come."

"It looks like we'll have to gate-crash after all," said Cora.

"Yes, please!" said Emily.

It was weird being in school at the weekend. They passed Mr B's classroom, where a group including Shanti's mum were sitting around tables, chatting and sewing costumes.

The sound of banging and hammering was coming from the main school hall further along the corridor. They hurried through the door. The hall was a very large room with high ceilings, a wooden floor, big windows and a stage at one end. Many years ago, it had been the only room in the school and all the classes had taken place in there with desks in rows, but over time, new, modern classrooms had been built as the school

had grown and expanded. Now the hall was now just used for assemblies, P.E. and putting on plays.

Emily's dad was in there constructing scenery along with a couple of other parents. Seeing the girls, he broke off from sawing a piece of wood and waved. "Hi, you lot."

Emily ran over and gave him a hug. "Hi, Dad. Thanks for coming and helping with this. Who's looking after the shop today?"

"Steph," said her dad. Steph was the assistant manager. "We're getting on well with making the scenery. The castle's done already and is out in the

playground, ready for painting. You can get on with designing and painting it if you want. There's some paint, brushes and dust sheets out there too."

"OK!' said Emily eagerly.

It was a sunny afternoon and the girls were happy to be outside. While Cora, Sophie and Shanti began painting the castle with a base-coat of golden paint, Emily sketched out a castle design on a piece of paper, drawing stone walls with pink roses clambering over them. She checked and then, when Mr B and her dad liked it and the base-coat had dried, she began transferring her design to the scenery, drawing it on in a soft pencil.

The others began to paint in the outlines of the stones and the branches of the roses. Emily did the harder bits, adding shading to the stones and painting in the delicate pink flower petals. Their arms and faces were soon covered with splashes of paint but nobody cared because they were having so much fun!

Mr B came into the playground holding a cardboard pizza box and some cans of lemonade. "Girls, Sophie's dad has just dropped off some pizzas and drinks for everyone." Sophie's dad was the manager of Franketelli's, the best Italian restaurant in town. "Have you worked up an appetite?"

"Yes!" they all said. Smelling the pizza, Emily suddenly realised how hungry she was.

Mr B set the pizza and drinks down and looked at the golden castle walls with the pink roses. "Oh. My. Goodness," he said, putting his hand to his chest. "It looks almost as beautiful as my real-life wedding venue."

"I modelled it on the hotel," Emily said with a smile.

"Emily did all the drawing and designing, we just painted the easy bits," said Sophie, handing around slices of pizza.

"You're a girl of many talents, Emily!"

Mr B looked at her and smiled. "I hear you've agreed to recite the poem for us at the wedding."

Emily gulped and nodded.

"She's a bit nervous about it," said Cora, taking a big bite of pizza.

"There's no need to be nervous!" said Mr B. "You'll be fine."

"But what if I forget the words?" Emily said anxiously, staring down at her drink.

Mr B waved his hand. "Then do what the best actors do – improvise! Sound confident and no one will ever know." His phone rang. He checked it and smiled. "It's your Uncle Mike."

The girls munched their pizza as Mr B

answered the phone call.

"Hello! . . . What?" The cheerfulness drained from Mr B's voice and his face grew serious. "No! When?" There was a pause. "But that's awful."

Emily gave her friends an alarmed look. What was going on?

Mr B sank down on the ground. "What are we going to do?" He covered his eyes with the hand not holding the phone. "This can't be happening! Yes, right, thanks for telling me, Mike. I'll see you later."

He ended the call and stared at his phone despondently.

"Mr B?" Sophie said.

"Is everything OK?" Emily asked anxiously.

"No, no, it's not." Mr B looked dazed. "Langton Hall has burned down!"

All her worries about saying a poem at the wedding ceremony flew out of Emily's head as she stared at Mr B's distraught face. "Burned down?" she echoed.

He nodded. "There was a fire in the kitchen. They thought it was a false alarm and didn't call the fire brigade quickly enough. The hotel is ruined – burnt to the ground."

"So, what are you going to do about the wedding?" Emily asked.

"We're going to have to cancel it," said Mr B helplessly. "Nowhere else will be available at such short notice. The wedding is off!"

Chapter Eight

"There has to be something we can do," Emily's mum said, looking at Uncle Mike and Mr B across the kitchen table that evening. "Surely, you don't have to cancel the wedding."

After telling the girls the awful news, Mr B had swallowed down his upset and

with a brave "the show must go on" he
had continued supervising the scenery
and costume-making until six o'clock
when everyone left. Then he and Emily
had driven back to her house. Mum,
Dave and Uncle Mike were waiting
there to talk about the wedding crisis.

"There must be a venue that's
available," said Dave.

"I've been ringing round all
afternoon," said Uncle Mike. "But
every place big enough to hold two
hundred guests is booked up. Thanks for
trying though, Emily." He gave Emily a
grateful look. After she and the rest of the
Bridesmaid Club had heard the news,

they had gone online and made a list of all the possible places to hold a wedding near Easton-on-Sea. They'd sent the list on to Uncle Mike, but it hadn't been any good.

"Couldn't you just get married in a registry office like I did?" said Mum.

"Or a restaurant like Franketelli's?" Emily suggested. "That's where Sophie's parents had their wedding reception."

"Not with two hundred people invited," said Mr B. "We can hardly just uninvite three-quarters of them. Some of your relatives are travelling all the way from Jamaica and most have already booked their tickets and hotels."

"There must be somewhere," said Dave.
"We just need to think outside of the box
— a football stadium? An ice rink?"

"They'd be big enough," agreed Uncle
Mike with a quick look at Mr B, who

groaned and put his head in his hands. "But they're not really us."

"We were going to have the perfect wedding," said Mr B. "A grand hotel, drinks and canapés in the rose garden, the ceremony in the beautiful old hall . . . It was going to be so dramatic! No, if we can't have a wedding we want then I'd rather wait until the hotel is rebuilt and redecorated."

Emily hated seeing her uncle and her uncle-to-be looking so upset. *If only I could think of a place where they could get married,* she thought longingly.

Her phone buzzed. Checking the screen, she saw that her dad had sent her

a photo of Sleeping Beauty's finished castle. He'd set the castle up on the stage before they left for the night and taken a photo of the Bridesmaids Club posing in front of it. His message said:

Thought this might cheer you up. You and the gang did a brilliant job at painting it. I'm sorry the wedding's been postponed and you've got to wait longer to be a bridesmaid. Love you lots, Dad xxx

Emily's forehead wrinkled as an idea wriggled its way into her head. Was it possible? Could it work?

"Put your phone away while we're at the table, Em," Mum said automatically.

But Emily didn't.
Instead, she
waved her
phone in
the air and
jumped to
her feet.
"I've got
an idea!" she
gasped. "I know
where you can get
married!" she said to Uncle Mike and
Mr B. "At school!"

"School?" they both repeated.

"Yes! In the hall! You said you wanted
to get married in a big old hall – well,

the school hall is big and old, and it can easily fit two hundred people." Her mind raced on. "We could get some silky fabric and drape it across the ceiling and have the castle from *Sleeping Beauty* as the backdrop. It would look amazing! You said it's good to improvise when things go wrong, Mr B, so how about improvising with this?" Excitement pumped through her. "What do you think?"

For once Mr B looked lost for words.

However, Uncle Mike was nodding enthusiastically. "It's a great idea! The school has a personal meaning for both of us because it's where we met, at the

summer fair two years ago. It would be lovely to have all our friends and family there. I wasn't fussed about having a fancy wedding venue anyway . . ." He looked at Mr B. "Alex, what do you think? I know you loved the hotel and if that's really where you want to get married then of course we can wait."

"Well . . ." Mr B said slowly.

Emily held her breath but then to her relief, Mr B's face split into a wide grin. "I think it's a GENIUS idea!" he declared, banging the table. "Emily, you've saved the day! School will be the perfect venue. I'll have to get permission from the head, but I'm sure she'll agree.

And I know the school has a marriage licence because an old pupil asked to get married there last year."

"You could have drinks in the playground," said Mum. "And a disco in the hall in the evening."

"But what about food?" said Uncle Mike. "We'll never find a caterer at this late date."

"What about that posh burger van that comes to the summer fair?" said Emily. "They might be free and their burgers are really yummy."

"Proper burgers not mini ones!" said Uncle Mike in delight. "I like that plan!"

"You could have lamb burgers, jerk

chicken burgers, veggie burgers and massive bowls of salad," said Mum.

"And I'd be happy to make the wedding cake," said Dave.

"As for the wedding itself, we could get married on the stage," concluded Mr B in delight. "What could be more dramatic than that? I can just see it now – our friends and family all gathered in the hall, us entering to music and approaching the stage—" He broke off and snapped his fingers. "Music! Emily, if we have the wedding at school, do you think everyone in the play would come along and sing at the ceremony? They could stay for the barbecue, too."

Emily gasped. "I bet they would!" Her thoughts whirled. If everyone from the show was going to be there, that would mean Sophie, Cora and Shanti could be at the wedding too!

"A wedding with a show choir!" exclaimed Mr B, grabbing Uncle Mike's hands and kissing him. "Now, that really *is* my dream wedding!"

Chapter Nine

The next week flew by in a whirlwind of activity. There were rehearsals every day at school and lots of frantic wedding planning afterwards. All sorts of things needed sorting out – the burger van and DJ for the disco had to be booked, suitable chairs and tables had to be hired

and there were decorations and wedding favours to make.

Every night after school, Emily's Bridesmaids Club friends came round to her house. They made metres of purple-and-gold bunting to hang around the playground and hall. Mr B wanted all the guests to have fancy candles as wedding favours so the girls spent one whole evening tying purple ribbons around the candles and another evening painting little ceramic hearts with the guests' names to use as place settings.

Dave was busy testing out recipes for the wedding cake, which was going to be a tower of the grooms' five favourite

types of cake – Jamaican ginger cake, lemon drizzle, carrot cake, pound cake and Red Velvet cake all covered with thick, smooth layers of white fondant icing. He showed the girls how to make beautiful purple and yellow flowers out of icing which he was going to use to decorate the five tiers.

While the girls were helping with the wedding preparations, they practised their lines over and over again until Emily began to feel she could say them in her sleep. Almost before she knew it, the day of the show had arrived.

"Are you nervous?" Mum said, walking her back to school after an early tea.

The cast had been asked to get to school at six to change into their costumes and have their make-up done before the performance started at seven.

"I am," admitted Emily. She could feel nerves building inside her. When they reached the school and she saw the rows and rows of chairs in the hall, her tummy clenched as if someone had grabbed it with a fist.

"Well, here we are," her mum said. "Good lu—"

"No!" Mr B greeted them outside of the hall. "You should never wish an actor good luck. Saying good luck brings bad luck. You have to say 'break a leg'!"

"OK then, well, break a leg," said Emily's mum, giving her a quick kiss. "Dave and I will be in the audience. Your dad is coming too."

Emily gulped as her mum left and she looked into the empty hall. Soon it would be full of people, and they'd all be staring at the stage. "This is it, Emily!" said Mr B. "The big night!"

"Yes." Her voice was as faint as a mouse's squeak.

Mr B frowned. "You sound nervous."

Emily nodded. "I am a bit," she admitted.

"Well, don't be," Mr B said firmly. "You've been doing wonderfully

in rehearsals this week. You haven't forgotten a single line."

"But what if I forget them when I'm on stage?"

Mr B smiled. "Here's a little tip that even professional actors use sometimes. If you start feeling nervous because everyone's watching you, look out at the audience and imagine them all sitting there in their underwear!"

Emily giggled.

"It works, I promise," he said, giving her a wink. "Now off you go to get changed."

Emily hurried to her classroom which was being used as the girls' dressing room

for the night. Cora, Shanti and Sophie were already there. Helena and a couple of the other mums were setting out make-up and brushes.

"Come on in," said Helena excitedly. "Let's get you into your costume and all made up."

A short while later, Emily stared at herself in the full-length mirror, astonished at the transformation. Helena had fixed her hair in an elaborate up-do and sprayed it with silver glitter. Emily's costume was a pale blue and Helena

had put sparkly blue eyeshadow on her eyelids to match and dusted her cheeks with silver and blue glitter. On her back she had large gauzy silver wings.

"You look amazing, Em!" called Sophie from where she was having her make-up done.

"Really beautiful," called Shanti.

"This is so much fun!" said Cora as she pulled on her biker boots. Her strawberry blonde hair had been slicked back and her eye make-up was dramatic – she had lots of purple eyeliner, black lipstick and sparkly gold glitter sprinkled across both cheeks.

I can do this, Emily thought, looking at

herself in the mirror. *At least I hope I can.*

All around her everyone was chattering excitedly and the room was thick with the smell of hairspray. They could hear the audience starting to arrive.

"Let's get a photo of you all now you're ready!" said Helena.

"I'm so nervous!" gasped Tilly as they got into line, though Emily didn't think she looked very nervous at all.

"Me too!" squealed Shanti. "I'll probably end up making up half of the words I'm singing."

Helena got them all into a row. "Say 'showtime'!" she said.

Everyone shouted it out and she took a photo with her phone.

"Great, well, it's almost time to get onstage," she said, checking the clock.

Emily tried to remember her first line but it had vanished from her head. She sat down and took a few deep breaths to calm herself.

"Are you OK?" asked Shanti.

Emily couldn't speak. Her mouth was as dry as sandpaper.

Just then there was a knock at the door. "Everyone respectable? Can I come in?" called Mr B.

"Yes, that's fine. Everyone's ready!" said Helena, opening the door.

Mr B came in, looking as if he was going to burst with excitement. "Five minutes and then it's time to walk on to that stage and shine like the stars you are. I'm so proud of you all and of the hard work you've put in. Don't let me down now."

"We won't!" everyone apart from Emily chorused.

"Right, into starting positions then please," said Mr B.

"I can't do this," Emily whispered to Shanti. She felt like she was about to be sick.

"Yes, you can," said Shanti, taking her hand and pulling her to her feet. She

glanced across the room and beckoned the others over. A few seconds later, Sophie and Cora were there beside Emily too. They seemed to realise how nervous she was feeling.

"You're going to be amazing, Em," Cora told her.

"If you do forget a line, don't worry, I'll whisper it to you," said Sophie.

"And you can always copy me if you forget the dance," said Shanti. "We're in this together, Em. There's no need to be worried. You're not on your own."

Seeing her friends' encouraging smiles, Emily felt her nerves fade slightly.

They made their way to the side of

the stage. "Ssh!" the teacher there hushed everyone. "OK, take your places."

They tiptoed on to the stage. The curtains were shut, but on the other side of them Emily could hear lots of voices laughing and talking. She peeped through a crack in the curtains and saw that the hall was packed, every seat taken. Then the three good fairy godmothers stood in a line at the back ready for the opening number, while Cora went to stand on the left-hand side of the stage until it was time for her to make a dramatic entrance.

"This is it!" hissed Sophie in excitement. "It's about to start!"

Emily's heart beat quickly as she stared at the curtains in terror. As the opening bars of the music started, the audience fell quiet and the curtains began to open.

The lights shining on to the stage were so dazzlingly bright that Emily could only see the first couple of rows of the audience. The rest of the hall was in darkness. Next to her, she felt Sophie and Shanti start to sway in time to the music and then they – and the rest of the cast – began to sing. For a moment, Emily froze as she stared at the people in the front row, but then she remembered Mr B's words. She pictured the audience sitting in their underwear and suddenly

she didn't feel so scared any more. She started to join in. Shanti and Sophie grinned at her and Cora gave her a thumbs up from the wings.

I can do this! Emily realised. Her singing got louder and more confident as she was swept up in the joy of performing. By the time the song had finished, the knots in Emily's stomach had loosened. She remembered all her lines in the first scene and after that the rest of the play passed in a blur. It was so much fun!

It was wonderful to hear the audience laughing at the funny moments and hearing them catch their breath as Shanti sang her solo, her sweet voice

soaring through the hall. It was brilliant to hear clapping after each song and it was even good fun when things went wrong, like a doorknob coming off in Cora's hand. She just waved it round in mock outrage and shouted, "I don't think much of this castle! You should get a carpenter in!"

Emily could hardly believe it when they reached the end. The audience gave them a standing ovation as they bowed, and someone even threw flowers on to the stage!

Afterwards, they sat down on the edge of the stage, buzzing with excitement and happiness as Mr B thanked all the

parents who'd got involved and thanked the cast again for their hard work. Then Tilly brought some flowers and a massive box of chocolates on stage for Mr B from the cast. She thanked *him* for all his hard work which made him get teary-eyed and choked up. Finally, the show was over.

"That was awesome!" Sophie said, hugging the rest of the Bridesmaids Club as they came off stage.

"The best play ever!" said Cora, her eyes shining.

"I wish we could do it all again!" said Shanti.

"Did you enjoy it, Em?" Cora asked.

Emily nodded, smiling from ear to ear. "Definitely! At the start I just wanted to run away, but I ended up loving it. Thank you for making me do it and for helping me with my nerves."

"We'll help you again at the wedding," promised Shanti.

A thrill ran through Emily when she

thought about the wedding! Now that she'd performed in the show, she realised she wasn't dreading saying the poem at the ceremony any more. She knew she could do it. In fact, she could hardly wait to be a bridesmaid with her four best friends at her side!

Chapter Ten

"How do I look?" Uncle Mike asked, coming down the stairs on the day of the wedding. He was dressed in a dark blue wedding suit with a lilac waistcoat, white shirt and purple tie.

"Very handsome," said Mum, smiling and coming forward to take his hands.

"Alex is going to be bowled over."

Emily blinked at her uncle through her glasses. It was odd to see him in a suit — he usually wore jeans and comic book T-shirts — but she had to admit he did look very smart. Her mum looked great too, in her elegant purple suit with a thin gold belt.

"Do you like my dress?" Emily said, spinning round so that the sparkly skirt of her lilac bridesmaid dress swirled out. Helena had done a wonderful job. It had thin straps embellished with tiny gems and layers of gauzy material that shimmered with gold flecks. The skirt reached all the way to the floor and

swished when Emily walked. Her mum
had bought her some gold ballet pumps
to wear, as well as a pale gold headband
for her hair.

Emily had sprayed the glitter spray
from the play lightly over her dark
black curls and then she'd put on a
bit of watermelon-flavoured lip-gloss
that Sophie had given her for her last
birthday. She was really pleased with
how she looked.

"I've never seen you look so beautiful,"
her mum said warmly.

Uncle Mike nodded. "And to complete
the look . . ." He held out a purple
jewellery box. "This is from Alex and

me to say thank you for being our wonderful bridesmaid."

Emily opened the box carefully. Inside there was a delicate silver bracelet. Her name was engraved on it. "Thank you!" she breathed. Her uncle helped her to slip it on and fasten it around her wrist. It looked really pretty.

They waited for the car that was going to take them all to the wedding. Uncle Mike paced around. "Where is it?" he fretted, checking his watch for the hundredth time. "Why isn't the car here?"

"It's not supposed to be here until two o'clock," soothed Mum. "It's not even five to yet. Relax, Mike."

But Uncle Mike didn't seem able to relax at all. He kept reading over the wedding vows he and Mr B had written to say at the ceremony.

At two o'clock on the dot, the smart black car arrived. It had purple and gold ribbons stretching from the wing mirrors to the bonnet. "Right, come on, let's go," said Uncle Mike.

He hurried them out into the car. Mum sat in the front and Emily sat in the back with Uncle Mike. "Are you OK?" she asked him softly. He looked really anxious.

"Yes . . . No . . . Oh, I don't know," he admitted, shaking his head.

Emily understood the look on his face. "Are you feeling nervous?"

"Not about getting married. I don't have any doubts about that," said Uncle Mike. "It's the service I'm worried about. Alex loves a crowd, so he'll be in seventh heaven. But I hate speaking in public. What if I freeze when I try to say my vows?"

Emily reached out and squeezed his hand. "I felt like that before the play but I got through it and managed to remember my lines. You'll be fine."

"Easy to say," Uncle Mike said, sighing.

"Mr B gave me a good tip," Emily said.

"He said that if you're feeling scared you should just imagine all the audience in their underwear."

Her uncle chuckled. "That's just the sort of thing Alex would say."

Emily leaned closer. "Well, guess what? It works!" she whispered. "I promise. And remember, I'll be with you for the whole of the service. If you're worried, just look at me."

He squeezed her hand. "Thanks, Emily," he whispered back. "You're the best."

When they reached her school, Emily gasped. All the wedding guests, including the cast of *Sleeping Beauty*, were lined up on the school drive to greet them. They waved and cheered as the car drove past.

"We're here! It's actually happening!"

said Uncle Mike, loosening his tie
slightly.

"It's going to go brilliantly," said
Emily firmly. "Trust me. After all, I'm the
bridesmaid."

The guests trooped into the hall and
found their seats. Then, as music played
softly, Mum, Emily and Uncle Mike
went up the aisle and on to the stage
where the wedding celebrant, a woman
called Brenda, was waiting for them with
a big smile. The stage lights illuminated
Sleeping Beauty's castle behind her. It
made the perfect backdrop.

Looking out into the audience, Emily saw her grandma smiling proudly and wearing a big pink hat. She had arrived from Jamaica a few days earlier and was staying at Uncle Mike's house. The Bridesmaids Club were sitting with the rest of the cast in the second row, ready to come on stage and sing at the end of the ceremony. Shanti, Cora and Sophie all grinned and waved at her. She smiled back at them.

Suddenly the music changed to a song called 'Don't Stop Believin''. The guests fell silent. The hall doors burst open and Mr B strode in. He was wearing a dark blue suit like Uncle Mike's but his

had a tailcoat and he was wearing a top-hat and had a lilac cravat around his neck instead of a tie. He stopped, threw his arms above his head, paused dramatically, then strode down to the aisle. He reached the stage, bounded up the steps and stopped opposite Uncle Mike.

The guests broke into a round of applause as both grooms beamed happily at each other.

The wedding was quite similar to the others Emily had been to in some ways. Brenda welcomed them all and then checked no one had any objections to Uncle Mike and Mr B getting married.

Then she asked them to come to the centre of the stage and say the vows they had prepared.

Emily, who was standing beside Uncle Mike, saw him swallow nervously.

"Underwear," she whispered to him.

A small smile caught at his mouth. Turning to give her a wink, he walked to the centre of the stage and took Mr B's hand. "Alex," he said, clearing his throat. "The moment I first met you at the school summer fair, I wanted to get to know you better. I'm so glad I did. You make me laugh, you encourage me, you challenge me, and you make me happier than I have ever been. I can't think of

anything I want more than to spend my life with you. I promise I will always look after you, care for you, be there for you . . ." He continued confidently until he reached the end of his vows.

Glancing at her mum, Emily saw happy tears shining in her eyes and, looking out at the audience, she saw other people dabbing tears away too. Uncle Mike had done it, he'd made his vows and he hadn't forgotten a single word! He gave Emily a relieved wink.

Alex didn't have any nerves at all. He loudly declared his love and promised to look after and care for Uncle Mike as long as he lived. They exchanged the

rings that Mum was holding and then the celebrant declared them married.

"We will now have a poem by William Shakespeare read by Emily, the bridesmaid," said Brenda. "Emily," she encouraged her forward.

Emily walked to the centre of the stage. She looked at her friends and at Mum and Dave, and knew they were all willing her on. She'd said her lines in the school play and she could say the poem now. Lifting her chin, she spoke the poem clearly without missing a single word. At the end everyone clapped.

"Thank you, Em. That was beautiful," Uncle Mike said, squeezing her shoulder

as she moved to stand beside him. Mr B
– now her Uncle Alex – looked close to
tears.

The guests rose and everyone sang a
song from *The Lion King* called 'Can You
Feel the Love Tonight'. Emily knew it
was Mr B's favourite musical. After that,
the cast from the play came on to the
stage, formed a line, and sang the grand
finale song from *Sleeping Beauty*. Then
it was time for Uncle Mike's favourite
reggae song, 'One Love' by Bob Marley.
By the end all the audience were on
their feet, joining in, and everyone on
stage was dancing as they sang.

"Mr B and your uncle look incredibly

happy together," said Cora.

"You were an amazing bridesmaid!" said Shanti, as they swung each other round.

"It's been the best day ever!" said Emily, her eyes shining as she saw her uncles busting some moves together.

"And there's still the barbecue to come!" said Sophie in delight.

Chapter Eleven

"I'm stuffed," groaned Cora. "But I'm determined to try all five layers of wedding cake."

The barbecue had been delicious. There had been as many burgers as people could eat, along with huge bowls of salad. Emily's grandma had

even made a special tropical salad with chicken, pineapple, and mangoes.

"I can't believe this is really the Bridesmaids Club's last wedding," Sophie said as they sat on the play equipment and munched on wedding cake. The cake with its five tiers and cascade of sugar flowers had drawn lots of admiring gasps. The cast from *Sleeping Beauty* were due to sing more songs from the show in a little while and then, after the singing, there was going to be a disco that would go on until midnight!

"I was so nervous about being bridesmaid and saying the poem, but now I'm sad it's almost over," said Emily.

Cora nodded. "It's been awesome being bridesmaids," she said.

"All the weddings we've been bridesmaid for have been so different," said Shanti.

"But they've all been brilliant," Sophie put in.

"I really don't want Bridesmaids Club to be finished," said Emily, with a rush of sadness. "I wish it could carry on."

"We'll always be best friends, even if we're not bridesmaids any more," said Sophie, linking arms with her.

"Always!" agreed Cora and Shanti.

"I wonder when Mr B wants us to sing again," said Cora.

"I'll go and check," said Emily. She headed over to where Mr B was standing next to her mum, with his arm round Uncle Mike. But before she could get there, Dave stepped in front of her. "Emily, could I borrow you for a sec? There's something I need to talk to you about."

"Sure," Emily said. She followed him to a quiet corner of the playground. "Is something wrong?"

"No, no," Dave said quickly. He shuffled his feet. Emily realised he looked nervous. "The thing is, coming here to this wedding and seeing how happy everyone is, it's made me think." Dave

took a deep breath. "I'd really like to get married to your mum. I love her – and I love you, too. I'd like to feel we are a forever family. Is . . . is that all right with you? If I ask for your mum's hand in marriage, I mean. Would it be OK if I became your step-dad?"

Happiness burst through Emily like a firework. "Yes! Yes! That's definitely OK with me!" She really liked Dave and she knew he made her mum happy.

Dave beamed at her. "Then I'll do it. I'll ask her right now!"

Emily caught her breath as he strode over to her mum. Turning, she raced back to her friends.

"Do we need to sing now?" asked Sophie.

Emily flapped her hands, almost too excited to speak. "Forget that!" she squealed. "It's my mum and Dave! He's going to propose to her! Come and see!" They all followed her and stopped just in time to see Dave drop down on one knee in front of Emily's mum.

"Brianna," he said, holding out a flower and gazing up at her as if she was the only person in the playground. "I think you are the most wonderful woman in the world and I would love to spend the rest of my life trying to make you as happy as you deserve to be.

174

I've spoken to Emily and she's OK with this, so please, will you agree to be my wife?"

Emily's mum looked shocked for a moment but then her face split into an enormous grin. "Of course I will, Dave. I'd love to marry you!"

Dave jumped to his feet, picked Emily's mum up and twirled her around. "You've just made me the happiest man alive!"

"No, that's me," said Mr B, smiling at Uncle Mike.

Emily and her friends jumped up and down in excitement as Dave kissed her mum.

"Your mum's getting married, Emily!"

said Shanti, clapping her hands.

"I know!" exclaimed Emily.

"Em?" Emily's mum called over breathlessly as Dave put her down. "I've got a question. Will you be my bridesmaid?"

"Yes!" Emily squealed. "Of course I will."

"We'll give you all the help you need," declared Sophie.

"We'll make sure your mum has the perfect day," promised Shanti.

Cora whooped. "You know what this means? Bridesmaids Club lives on!"

Emily felt a wave of happiness sweep over her. Another wedding to help organise. Another chance to be a bridesmaid. What in the world could be better than that?

The four friends held hands and they spun round, laughing. "Bridesmaids Club for ever!" they cried.

The End

Have you read **Beach Wedding Bliss** yet?
See where Bridesmaids Club began!

Posy Diamond

Bridesmaids Club

Beach Wedding Bliss

"Finished at last!" Sophie said, shutting her maths book in relief.

Her mum was standing at the sink, scrubbing potatoes for supper. "Homework done?"

Sophie nodded and pushed her blonde ponytail back over her shoulder. She was in Year Six at Crosshills primary school. It was great being at the top of the school – she just didn't like all the homework!

Max, her nine-year-old brother, was colouring in a poster. "I've almost finished my homework too," he said.

"Let's see." Sophie leaned over the table. It was a poster advertising their town. Max had drawn a picture of the seafront and the little promenade with the row of shops and restaurants that looked out on to the beach. Under it he'd written the words: Come to Easton-on-Sea! It SHORE is the place to be!

"It's really good," said Sophie, admiring the detail. "Is that Mr Franketelli sitting outside his restaurant?"

"Yep," said Max. Franketelli's was their family's favourite place to eat. It served the best pizzas ever! Mr Franketelli was old now and spent much of his time sitting under the green-and-white stripy awning outside the restaurant.

Sophie got up to help Mum with

supper and spotted her baby sister, Lucie, pulling a sieve out of an open cupboard. Sophie hurried over. "No, that's not a toy, Lu-lu!" Lucie was just over a year old and super cute, with pale blonde hair and wide eyes, the same sky-blue as Sophie and Max's.

"Mine!" Lucie said firmly, her pudgy hand tightening on the handle. She put the sieve on her head and smiled. "Hat!"

Sophie giggled. "It's a very nice hat, Lucie. Now, why don't you come and sit in your high chair with your hat, and leave the cupboard alone?" She scooped her sister up off the floor.

"Thanks, Sophie," said her mum,

throwing her a grateful look. "We really have to fix some child locks on the cupboards now that she's walking."

Sophie kissed her sister's soft hair. When Mum and Dad had first told her and Max they were going to have a baby sister, Sophie hadn't been too keen on the idea. But now she couldn't imagine life without Lucie. "Shall I get her a rice cake?"

"Yes, please. That'll keep her quiet while I get these potatoes in the oven," said Mum.

"What time will Dad be home?" Sophie asked, as she fetched Lucie a rice cake. Dad managed The Wellington, a

smart restaurant in town. He worked
very long hours, but he usually tried
to be home between shifts for an early
dinner with the family. Her mum worked
hard too – she was an accountant – but
she was able to do quite a lot of her
work from home.

"Soon," said Mum. "He's taking the
night off."

"Why?" Sophie was surprised. Her dad
almost never took a night off, apart from
on Mondays when the restaurant was
closed.

Mum tucked her blonde hair behind
her ears. "It's our anniversary."

Sophie was confused. "But you're not

married," she said. Her parents had never married, something she really didn't understand. *Who wouldn't want a wedding?* Sophie had been to one when she was six. She remembered the two bridesmaids wearing long pink dresses, lots of dancing and funny speeches. It had been such a happy day. But her parents had always said they didn't need a big day to prove their love. "How can you have an anniversary if you're not married?" Sophie asked.

"It's the anniversary of when we first met." Mum's eyes took on a far-away look. "It was fifteen years ago today on the beach." As she spoke, the back door opened and Dad walked in – broad-shouldered, dark-haired, blue eyes twinkling.

"Fifteen years!" he declared. "And I've loved every single one of them!" He swept Mum up in a hug and kissed her.

"Ew! Gross!" Max pretended to be sick. But Sophie grinned. She liked the fact that her parents were obviously still in love.

"Dada! Dada!" shouted Lucie, banging the sieve on her high chair table.

Dad walked over and scooped her out. "Fifteen years – so, tonight, my lovely family, we are going out to celebrate. I've booked us a table at Franketelli's."

Sophie squealed and Max whooped. "Pizza time!"

Mum looked anxious. "It's a nice idea, Tom, but I thought we agreed we wouldn't spend any extra money right now?" Sophie knew her parents were worried that The Wellington might close. If that happened, her dad would lose his job.

"It's just one meal," Dad said. "Come on, Lizzie."

Mum frowned. "But—"

"Juicy tomatoes and creamy mozzarella," Dad interrupted. "Plump olives, crispy pizza bases, meatballs oozing with sauce . . ."

"Home-made ice cream!" Max added. "Oh, please say we can go, Mum?"

"I-scream!" Lucie squealed.

Sophie put her hands together as if begging. "Please, Mum!"

Dad carried Lucie over and gave Mum a kiss on the cheek. "You have to say yes, Lizzie. How can you resist?"

The corners of Mum's mouth lifted into a smile as she gave in. "All right then. Yes!"

Half an hour later, the family parked their old blue people carrier and piled out in front of the restaurant. Mr

Franketelli was sitting outside as usual, enjoying the last few rays of the summer sun. His face was deeply wrinkled, his hair grey, but his eyes lit up when he saw the Jenkins family.

"*Buono sera,* my friends!" he said, getting up from his chair and opening his arms wide. "Welcome! Welcome! It is so lovely to see you again!" He spoke with a strong Italian accent.

Mr Franketelli kissed Mum on both cheeks, asked Dad about his work and then showed them to their table. The restaurant had been open for many years and was always busy. The walls were covered with photographs of southern Italy, where Mr Franketelli had been born. The red carpet was old and faded, and the green paint on the walls scuffed. But it didn't matter, because the restaurant smelt delicious and the chequered tablecloths were cheery. As usual, there was a pot of breadsticks in the centre of their table.

Max took one and wielded it like a weapon. "Gimme some dough!" he said to Dad.

"Or what? You wanna *pizza* this?" Dad grabbed another breadstick for a sword-fight.

"Remind me how many children I have again?" Mum said to Sophie, shaking her head.

The family sat down and ordered. Soon they were tucking into bowls of meatballs and homemade pasta for Mum and Dad, margarita pizza for Max and Sophie, and breadsticks and vegetables for Lucie.

To find out what happens next, read **Beach Wedding Bliss!**

Bridesmaids Club

Making wedding dreams come true!

Beach Wedding Bliss

Big Bollywood Wedding

Fairytale Wedding Wish

Wedding Day Drama